I0651131

The
Girl Who Could Walk
Through Walls

Solve more mysteries with the Conways in

When Kitty Met the Ghost

By Ernest G Mardon & Austin A. Mardon

And check out:

The Findhorn Monster
Early Saints and Other Saintly Stories for Children

The Girl Who Could Walk Through Walls

Ernest George Mardon
&
Austin Albert Mardon

Edited by Pauline Balogun

Golden Meteorite Press
Edmonton, 2012

A Golden Meteorite Press Book.

© 2012 copyright by Austin Mardon, Canada. All rights reserved. No part of this work may be reproduced in any form or by any means, electronic or mechanical, including photocopying, recording, taping, or any retrieval system, without the written permission of Golden Meteorite Press at aamardon@yahoo.ca. First Edition published in 1991. Printed in Alberta, Canada. Interior formatting and cover design by Alexa L. Guse, 2012

Published by Golden Meteorite Press.
126 Kingsway Garden
Post Office Box 34181,
Edmonton, Alberta, CANADA.
T5G 3G4

Austin Mardon
Telephone: 1-(780)-378-0063
Email: aamardon@yahoo.ca
Web site: www.austinmardon.org

Library and Archives Canada Cataloguing in Publication

Mardon, Ernest G., 1928-
The girl who could walk through walls / Ernest George
Mardon & Austin Albert Mardon ; edited by Pauline Balogun.

ISBN 978-1-895385-43-4

I. Mardon, Austin A. (Austin Albert) II. Balogun, Pauline
Jessica, 1994- III. Title.

PS8576.A6463G57 2011   C813'.54   C2011-905970-3

Contents

PAGE 01   LOCATION   STATE 041622Z
||
Action K — 12
Info co-03 ISO-CP C
R   413172MAY 53   MCH 48

FM MNST INT TEULINGS
TO BRTEMBASSY

TOPSEC   HAGUE 3954
SUBJECT: LION'S DEN

H PASS: AMBASSADOR / COS ME

For the recovery of a national treasure lost during the Rotterdam Blitz, we extend our sincerest thanks to the Conways, in particular Miss Katherine Conway for bravery in the face of danger and the risk of her personal safety to retrieve our heritage.

The Dutch Queen Wilhelmina personally extends her thanks to the Conways for the return of our national treasure and for their protection of Dutch Jews during the war.

DIRECTOR TEULINGS

Chapter One

"A letter has arrived for you, Sir," James said.

Arthur Conway glanced up from his paper at his manservant before returning his attention to the news.

"Very well, James. Who's it from?" Arthur said and set aside his newspaper, reaching for the tea James had brought in. He took a sip and gave his manservant a hard glance.

James' expression did not change.

"It doesn't say, Sir. It was left with a blank calling card on the hall table."

Arthur scowled. "Fetch me the card at once," he barked. He got up suddenly, his hip catching the edge of the table and knocking his teacup to the floor. It shattered into a thousand pieces on the rug.

"My apologies, Sir. Let me get that."

"Leave it. Get out and bring me that card." Arthur paced back and forth from the window, the letter still unopened in his hand.

James gave a quick bow and left to retrieve the card, but although he was sure he had not moved it, he couldn't find it. After several minutes of fruitless hunting, he returned to Arthur Conway, who had since opened the letter and was reading it.

"You have it?" Arthur asked looking up. Noticing James' empty hands, he continued without letting James answer, "What? Where is it?"

"It is not where I left it, Sir." James said, shifting his weight nervously.

"Unless it has legs, a card does not simply disappear. Get everyone to hunt for it. Look everywhere. I'll expect to have it in my hands upon my return."

"Should I pack your bags—"

"No, I am only going out for a few hours in the car. Tell Kitty that I shall be back in time for supper and that Charles and his friend are arriving this afternoon. Send my apologies, but this business is not the kind that can be put off."

"Yes, Sir. Your orders shall be carried out precisely. Should I call the car, sir?"

"No, I'll get it myself." With that he left his amazed servant staring after him.

"I wonder what could be the matter to make him go off like this," James mused to himself. "I had better not worry Miss Katherine or she'll take matters into her own hands."

He started for the door then noticed the envelope lying on the floor. 'Mr. A. Conway, M.O.R.' James hadn't the faintest idea what the letters meant. The return address was listed as Strong Gate Manor, de Moor Norfolk, England, and it had been posted in London eight days ago. James had nearly thrown it away when he noticed an odd stain on the back of the envelope. He brought it into the light and choked back a cry of horror. It was blood.

"James, what are you doing here? What's that in your hand?"

Chapter 1

"Nothing of consequence, Mistress Katherine. I—I...that is..."

Katherine 'Kitty' Conway ignored James' stammers with a toss of her golden tresses and plucked the envelope out of his hands. She was puzzled by the unfamiliar handwriting and she felt the sun of her happy, carefree soul darken with a sense of coming danger. She looked up at James, who looked distressed.

"Where is my father? Has something happened?"

"Nothing of the sort, Miss. He was called away on business, but he will be back for supper. He also mentioned that Mr. Charles Devonport and his friend will arrive in the afternoon. He sends his apologies that he won't be here himself."

Kitty stopped listening, still concerned about the envelope. Something wasn't right. Her father had told her just this morning that he was too busy with work lately and was going to take a well-earned rest at Storm Gate Manor, an old manor house in the middle of the Fens. All she did know was that she had to get to the bottom of it. James saw the look on her face and told her that the letter had been written in pencil, not ink, and that the white card that had arrived with it was missing. Kitty gave a soft word of dismissal and James departed, retreating to the kitchen where he told the staff to keep an eye out for the white card.

He returned to Arthur's study where he cleaned up the broken china before carrying out his duties. For a rare moment, he found himself without anything to attend to, so James retired to his sitting room and promptly fell asleep in his easy chair.

Not so with Kitty; She worried over her father's sudden departure. Added to that, was the destruction of her flower garden. Some creature —most likely a rabbit— had eaten the blooms off her best flowers. She had worked hard to keep her furry foe out of her pretty flower garden. It was the only thing a proper lady could do, especially in a place like this.

With a sigh, Kitty set about the house wandering from her room upstairs then to the garden and onto the dining room. By the time she had reached the library, Kitty felt too bored to even feign interest in a book.

"It is a lovely, old house," she told herself crossly, but knew that age and beauty were rarely, if ever, amusing.

At lunch, she ate nothing and spent the entirety of the afternoon doing as she had in the morning. Everything was so still and quiet that Kitty wondered if the servants had gone fishing or some such nonsense. There was nothing to do. Not a soul moved anywhere over the flat countryside, not one fox or bird to be seen. In the distance, Kitty noticed the proud white lines of a sailing yacht and immediately felt a desire to be on it and sailing out on the water. But there was nothing she could do to be on it, so she continued to be bored in a way unique to the wealthy. Come four in the afternoon, she was both tired and cross, nearly unable to string a pleasant thought together for anything in the world.

Her saving grace was the sound of a racer on the drive. Complete with squealing brakes and crunching gravel, it came to a stop beside the front stoop.

A moment later, the car door banged open and the laughter of Charles and Paul, family friends from Scotland Yard, tumbled out the car and drifted in through the sitting room window to Kitty's ears. Kitty didn't bother rising to greet them at the door, opting to remain sitting in the deep armchair as the two gentlemen were ushered in.

"Good afternoon, my fair Lady," Paul said in his most gracious tone. "It is truly a remarkable day in these parts. Why, the heat alone would leave me half-dead were it not for the rejuvenating promise of your company. That and the fool your father trusts his money with." Paul continued his one-sided banter as he fell into the nearest chair and fanned himself with his hat. "Really, Charles, was there any need to drive like a madman when even going sixty barely created the illusion of a breeze? Driving all the way out here from London on the most rottenly hot day is really utterly cruel."

Chapter 1

Charles ignored Paul's tirade. "Good afternoon, Miss Conway." Charles said softly, his quiet voice managing to carry over Paul's continued complaints. "I was sorry to hear in your telegram that those pests are back again. I hope they didn't cause too much damage."

A faint colour blossomed in Kitty's cheeks at his words. Leave it to Charles to find a way to embarrass her discreetly. She could have knocked him in the head for announcing such things when Paul was in hearing. She had telegrammed him that morning to get him to bring some potted plants to replace the ones that had been eaten.

Paul picked up on the topic immediately, never one to miss a joke however bad or in poor taste, "Honestly, I don't understand the riff-raff these days. I would have gone for the begonias. They clash with the brickwork so."

A book flying across the room stopped him short. It missed the mark, or not, depending on who was asked.

"Oh, come now, Kitty. You might have hurt me and then how would I play with pet rabbit?"

"It is hardly my pet and if you say so again, I—I…" Kitty broke off, words failing her. She had been cross all afternoon, but now she was near irate.

Charles noticed the dangerous gleam in her eye and quickly moved to diffuse the situation. "Kitty, dear, I haven't seen your father yet. He still hasn't confirmed if he wants to invest in that cruise line. And I have some mail for him here."

"He has gone off somewhere with the car, although goodness knows where."

"I, for one, would not leave this place for all the riches in the world, not with a chair like this. Bunny and I will have all the rest we want and he can have all the flowers he wants—if he likes them, as I am sure he will. They must be a splendour to behold or he would not bother eating them. Yes, we shall have a lovely time here."

"And you can have it all by yourselves, too. Good riddance!" Kitty cried as she leapt to her feet. Something had just occurred to her. "I really must depart, gentlemen. No, Charles," she added, noting his building protest, "I am as cross as an old biddy and would hardly make good company for our two young heroes." With a light laugh, she ran out of the room.

A minute later, they heard the car starting.

"That car is too difficult for a girl to drive," Charles cried, spring to his feet in great alarm. "She won't be able to control it. Even I find it difficult to turn that wheel! I've never even taken her out in it. What will her father say?"

"Oh, she's all right. Don't fuss," Paul said. They both knew that the car had been acting up their entire trip, but bringing such a matter up wouldn't change Kitty's mind, so it was best left unsaid.

They had a long time to wait and during it, they cornered James. What he had to say about the morning's excitement did nothing to hearten them. There was nothing to do, but wait. Come eight o'clock, however, and they both went to the phone. Paul rang up the police to incite them into action while Charles waited for one of the missing Conways to call.

The police were dispatched, put at Paul's disposal. He and Charles departed immediately, silent and tense. They drove far and wide, covering more distance than they had earlier thought possible. Come daybreak and no one had heard from the missing person.

The morning went by with no better results, but in the afternoon, their hunt reaped its reward.

Paul sat in the passenger seat, eating raisins from a paper bag when Charles stopped the car and turned to him excitedly. He demanded to know the day of the month, to which Paul replied that it was the twenty-fourth of August, a Sunday.

At once, Charles' face fell.

Chapter 1

"What was it?" Paul asked.

"Well, as a matter of fact, I thought that they might have gone over to Holland to get in touch with an old friend. He wrote some time ago that they should visit him in the third week of August, but I suppose it is too late, of course."

He turned back to the wheel and was about to drive off when he noticed something peculiar about the truck in front of them. It was very obviously a delivery truck from Holt, with even a kind of plant stuck to it that was only found in Holt, yet here it was nowhere near Holt. That wasn't unusual in of itself, but lorries rarely drove about on a Sunday without any cargo.

"I've been waiting for a break, same as you, but if the ever-changing look on your face tells me anything, it's that we've found it." Paul calmly murmured, patting the weapon in his pocket.

The lorry eventually slowed next to a short dock in a nearby village and a man hopped in off a sailboat, giving Charles and Paul a cursory glance. In the moment he did so, they both immediately recognized him as George Stateman, the man who had sworn revenge on the Conways.

"So our old friend turns up, right when Arthur and Kitty disappear. I say, Charles, let's go for a drive and see if we can't catch us a whopper this time."

Charles had already started to tail the vehicle. In a short time, they had left the village behind and were driving across the countryside towards Dark Gate. It was hard to follow a vehicle surreptitiously to the middle of nowhere, especially when no one else seemed interested in going to that particular plot of empty. So when the lorry stopped abruptly in the middle of the road and four armed men piled out, neither Charles nor Paul were particularly surprised.

"Well, we're trapped," Paul sighed, glancing at the car pulling up behind them. "I think it would be best if one of us splits while the other sees what these fellows are up to in person."

"I think you'd best be doing the smooth talking to the captors bit. I always end up shouting. Sorry to dump this on you again, mate. It's best if we stick to what we know."

"It's alright, chap. Don't get yourself done in." The two friends grasped hands and with that, wished each other good luck.

George didn't seem concerned with the well-being of the men down the road from him as he started shooting right away. His aim, and his luck, were true and Charles was hit.

Paul saw red and started emptying his own gun as he ran out into the road, running full speed towards the nearby woods.

But it was too late. Before he knew it, his gun was empty and the men were upon him. All he knew was that something hit him across the side of his head and his world went black.

Charles had marginally better luck. The bullet had only grazed his arm, but the wound was bleeding badly. In the time Paul made a distraction, Charles got to his feet and dove across the hedges into the wheat field. He managed to make quite a ways into the field before Paul was subdued. He heard George order his men to get him and doubled his efforts to escape.

"We must get him, you fools! He is the only one with any brains and you let him slip through the net! You scum had better get him or you'll be joining him on the other side one way or another!"

Stateman's men quickly pushed past their leader and fired into the field. Charles fell flat on his face. He had no wish to see who would win in a bone-versus-copper showdown. He scrambled forward on his stomach, crawling along as fast as his bleeding arm would allow. He heard George scream at his men to run into the field after him.

"He can't be far. He can hardly walk. Follow his trail and get him. Shoot him dead or drag him back here. I don't care!"

They needed no second bidding; The way George held his gun

would make any man wish to be farther away. Charles cleared the field and wiggled through the hedge with some difficulty. There lay another field ahead with yet another hedge on the far side. Charles thought quickly; He wouldn't make it in his condition, not with his enemies almost upon him.

He looked left and right. There was only wheat as far as the eye could see, save a grove of trees a dozen yards away. It only took a moment for him to cover the distance.

The difficulty was getting up the tree with his arm the way it was and then stay there until it was safe to come down. He managed the first in what he believed to be record time. It wasn't a moment too soon because as soon as he pulled his legs up under him, George's men rushed through the hedge with a shout.

Upon seeing the undisturbed wheat fields, the men started searching the area, namely where Charles had been only moments before.

"Maybe he didn't get hit after all," one of the men grumbled, "He's gotten away, I'm sure."

"Impossible!" George roared, finally catching up with his lackeys. "I got his arm for sure. He has to be nearby."

"Well, he might be, but the police have been driving around and if they catch us looking around all funny, they'll want to know what we're up to. I say we forget about him. It's the middle of nowhere and he's shot with no supplies at all. I say, let nature take her course. He won't last the night."

George didn't like the idea, but he saw the sense of it and gave the order to return to the cars. In a short while, the sound of their voices died away in the still summer air, leaving Charles to his bitter thoughts.

"Oh, well," he half-said, "I'm still at large and they aren't looking for me, which means I can look for Kitty and Mr. Conway, in peace. I wonder where they got to. And where's Paul? I've got to find them, even if it takes the rest of my vacation days for the year."

Charles managed to get out of the tree without incident, but when he looked over the hedge, he saw that the cars and lorry were still sitting on the road. He scrambled back to the protection of the grove, hoping that if the men came back, they wouldn't be looking too hard. He hadn't slept and the pain in his arm was making it hard to concentrate. Even in the shade of the tree, the afternoon sun was mercilessly hot and Charles slipped out of consciousness without even realizing.

Hours passed and it was only the setting sun in his eyes that finally woke Charles. He jerked awake, not quite steady on his legs, but set off for the nearest town, hoping to get to the bottom of things before long.

Chapter Two

She sat up and rubbed her neck and the back of her head, belatedly noting that it was both extremely tender and sore to the touch.

"Where—how did I get here?" She asked the blackness around her, bleary and a hair shy of passing out again.

With a sudden jerk, remembrance clawed its way into Kitty's thoughts, sending a chill straight into her bones. It was all so clear, so frightening, that she sorely wanted to fall back into a faint or perhaps bash her head against a wall until her mind lost its grasp of the facts. If only it were not for the sharp throb in the back of her skull, she might even go to sleep, but no such luck exists.

Kitty put her head on her knees and thought deeply. She couldn't remember the larger details. Had it been yesterday or was it still today when she had left the house in Charles' yellow racer?

She looked at her watch, feeling its presence rather than seeing it. Charles had given it to her for her last birthday. Somehow, it had stopped working and even the face had come off. She felt like crying, but decided against such a blatant show of self-pity. The only thing was to get out of this place and get on with it, but first, she needed to get the story straight in her own mind.

She had left the house, intending only to go so far as the nearest village, but upon arriving there, the day had proved too pleasant and she had continued driving farther and farther away. Somehow, she ended up deep in the Fens and the road had turned into a track.

Kitty told herself to turn around then, but a glance at her watch informed her that the hour was still young and she did not have the curfew of a hapless schoolgirl. She got out of the car.

There was still plenty of time left to return and the view was truly one-of-a-kind. It would be a shame to leave without taking in the full glory of the sky and the flat country, and the sound of the rolling surf with the high sails of boat drifting past her. She could even make out the men on deck, getting the ship in order. She thought it odd that such a large boat would sail so close to the Fens. If they got stuck, there was no telling when they'd be able to get out again.

At last, Kitty decided it was time to return. It was either go back or spend a sleepless night scratching gnat bites.

She put her foot on the starter.

Nothing happened. She tried again with the same results. She stared at the dash. She was out of gas.

"Of all the rotten luck! Why didn't Charles tell me he was out of petrol? Now, I'm stuck out here and the nearest village is miles away! It looks as though I shall have to walk back. Oh well, nothing like a brisk evening walk to get the spirits up." She said cheerfully. She took long, swinging strides back down the road.

The boat completely slipped her mind or she would have gone to them for help. As it were, her thoughts were completely preoccupied with a certain visitor of hers whom she hoped was also in good spirits.

She would have remained happily in her thoughts were it not for the sudden appearance of a large, half-starved man.

"A grand evening, isn't it?" Kitty asked the man.

The man's whole frame seemed to go weak at her words.

Chapter 2

"Miss," he cried, "I am not as bad as I look. Please, for God's sake, help me get away from them."

"From whom?! And what would I be saving you from?"

"Nothing and no one that can send me to prison," the man grew pale and agitated. "It's too late, it is. They have me. Don't let them take me!" And he reached out towards her before collapsing at her feet.

"I promise I won't," Kitty swore, staring at her curious, new acquisition. It was then that she heard the rough voices of men and the sound sent a chill through her body.

The man groaned at her feet, "Go before they take you too."

"As if they would dare even think such a thing."

"That's what you think, Miss," purred a rasping voice behind her.

Kitty spun around to come face-to-face with two men dressed as sailors. With a defiant tilt of her chin, Kitty spoke.

"It would be wise of you, gentlemen, to remove yourselves from my path."

"She thinks we're 'gentlemen,'" one of the men sneered.

"Listen here, Miss. That man is our prisoner and unless you stand aside, you'll be joining him in our brig."

"You will not lay one finger on me or you'll be sorry for it," Kitty said, taking out the pistol she kept on her person at all times. She might not be a hapless schoolgirl, but that didn't mean she was stronger than your average woman was.

The men exchanged looks before breaking down in raucous laughter.

"Do you hear that, Jack?" The second man held his sides. "It's a special kind of ma'am that carries around one of them toys—the kind of ma'am that can't really be called a lady, that is."

Kitty's blood was boiling and if the men had known any better, they'd have stopped there and gone on their way.

Jack walked up, gave Kitty a wink and swung his leg hard into the fallen man's side.

That was the last straw.

Kitty closed her eyes and pulled the trigger.

There was a cry of pain as Jack fell with his thigh gushing thick, red blood in great spurts.

"Get that bitch, Bill!" Bill hardly needed the command, going straight for Kitty's legs. Within a moment, Kitty was fighting Bill's grip in vain, unable to break free.

"You ask for trouble, girl, then you best know how to deal with trouble, I reckon," he growled as he pushed her down, squeezing her neck.

"We will teach you manners."

Kitty's head lolled to the side and the man let go with some surprise.

"Damn. Is she dead?" Bill gave Kitty a kick before turning to his partner. Jack had managed to press his jacket over his wound and tie it around his leg, but he didn't look too good.

"Do I look like a doctor? We'll have to bring the body in either case. We'll worry about getting rid of her later. The chief will already be ticked. We might as well get this right."

"Not that you will."

Both men turned around from tying up the unconscious man and tried not to swear too loudly; Standing in front of them was Kitty, a little flushed and dusty, but her hands were steady and her aim true. She wouldn't miss.

"You move and I will kill you. Don't doubt it," Kitty all but screamed.

They obeyed her this time. Their hands were above their heads within seconds.

Kitty examined her new captives. "Now what do I do with you?"

"Nothing," said a voice behind her. The next moment something hard slammed down on the back of her head and everything had gone black.

Now she was here, stuck in the inky darkness. Yet she was determined not to stay there. For what felt like an hour, Kitty felt the walls and floor of her cell. The walls were made of wood, but the floor was made of stone. It really was odd when she thought about it. It could be a cellar in a big manor somewhere, but it was rather small for that. She didn't hear anything and her attempts at breaking the wooden door only made the silence more profound.

She sat down on the sack on the floor, wondering about the man in rags, about Charles and her father, as well as Paul, and what they would do when she didn't return.

"I only hope they save me before I freeze to death or start eating unmentionable things to survive." Kitty recalled the contents of her pockets and hoped that she had forgotten a snack of some sort inside one. There was a fountain pen, a letter, some cards, half-eaten chocolate, a powder compact, some nails, and a nail file.

Kitty considered the objects for some time before selecting the nail file and heading to the door. She got down on her knees and stuck the file into the lock, not pushing it all the way in yet.

She then selected the card and slipped it under the door. With trembling fingers, she eased the file farther in and with a deafening clank, the key slipped out of the lock and onto the floor. With an inner cry of triumph, Kitty swiftly tugged the card towards her and made her way out of the cell.

It was not a moment later when she heard a man's voice. He was talking about showing off his prisoner.

Kitty stood there and let the sounds of the men come closer and closer. She could already see the thin beam of light from their torch. She ran to the corner by the stairs and pressed herself flat against the floor. She held her breath, fearing that even the tiniest noise would give her away.

The two men came nearer and nearer.

"Hey, mate," the man with the light said, "the door is open. Little girl must have gotten it open somehow, but she's still down here. We would have met her on the stairs otherwise."

They passed her. With luck, she might still get her freedom and reunite with her dad. The men entered the cell.

"We can't stay here too long. I took the keys off the hall table and the chief will be angry if he hears that we came down here to fool with the girl."

"Hey, what was that?"

"Don't mind the door, mate. Place is damn drafty. You can't keep nothing open."

Which would have been true, except it had been Kitty locking them both in before running upstairs as fast as she could.

There was a furious shout from behind. It only made her go faster. It was only a moment, but eventually Kitty looked at the kind of house she was in. It didn't look any different from any other house she had been in. All the doors were closed. She heard talking coming from the kitchen and decided to dump the keys on the hall table. There was a newspaper on the table as well, addressed to a 'Mr. May House, Sunny Place, Holt, Norfolk.'

It was dated August twenty-fourth. The slant of the light from the window told Kitty it was late afternoon. She'd been unconscious for the better part of a day, at least. She thought it was a wonder that she was awake at all, given the way the back of her head throbbed. No gentleman would have dealt such a cowardly blow, especially not to a lady.

I wonder who it was, she thought.

As if in answer to her question, the voice of a man drifted in from the direction of the garden: "That must be her."

Kitty could hear his steps as he walked down the narrow hallway towards her. She looked around wildly to find a place to hide. She did the only thing she could and without a second thought, slipped into a coat lying across a small table. When Dan Gray came into sight, he saw standing in front of him a girl of middle size wearing a brown coat, a pair of large glasses, and a scarf over her hair.

"Good evening. You are new, aren't you? I don't recognize your face."

Kitty fixed her best smile on her face, "I just arrived."

"I understand that Miss Smith," he continued with a nod, "could not accompany you. Please extend our thanks to her for sending you in her place."

"I only hope that I am suitable," Kitty added, wondering what she had gotten herself into this time.

"Oh, I wouldn't worry about that. I think you will do splendidly. Do come this way; you must be famished after your trip. London, was it?"

"Thank you, I appreciate it."

"It's good that you came straight here. We wouldn't want to let on the police that we have reinforcements, now would we?" Gray turned to give her a smile, but as he took in her condition, it became edged with concern. "Are you all right? You don't look well."

"Oh yes, I am just a tad faint. It has been dreadfully warm."

"Oh, but surely the train wasn't too terrible?"

"I'm afraid I have a sensitivity. It's nothing to be alarmed by. A bit of air and I'm right as rain."

"I'm glad you're well. For one awful moment, I was afraid I'd caught myself a spy, but I doubt the police would send such a lovely girl into harm's way. You can rest up a bit, but don't take too long since we have to be cleared out in an hour or so. You're welcome to anything in the kitchen, if you can find something," he said, gesturing airily about the kitchen. There were dirty, broken dishes piled everywhere.

"It'll be good to have someone with a knack for cooking and the like around. Mary wasn't much of a hand at it all." With that, he departed.

Kitty stared after him. He had been pleasant enough and easy to talk to. His face was nice enough, but he wasn't handsome by any stretch of the imagination. He didn't have the look of a criminal though, and Kitty was sure that he was not a killer, or the man who had struck her. She shook her head. Now was not the time for this. She wasted no more time in judging Gray and set about getting a decent meal. Her stomach complained with such force, it felt as though she had not eaten for years.

She gathered together whatever she thought was edible and just as she had constructed something resembling food, who but Bill would come in—the very same Bill that had threatened her at the beginning of this mess. He didn't look up at her, but proceeded down the hall. Kitty's hunger left her and she decided that it was high time she made her escape. She was pushing her luck enough as it was. Supposedly, she was a girl sent by a Miss Smith from London to help a house full of dangerous persons, two of which had attacked her and locked her up. She nearly made it to the back door when a presence behind her caused her to stop short.

Daniel Gray blew into the room, his face the colour of paper and his breathing shallow and erratic.

"Come on," he said, shaking, "the chief's car is waiting and we need to make a run for it. Pete and Tom have snitched to the police and they'll be here any minute now."

"But wha—"

"Now!" he said, grabbing her arm and dragging her out into the hall and out the front door.

"It was luck that we managed to grab Arthur Conway earlier today, but we have no choice but to leave the task of getting the daughter to those fools." Gray's grip tightened and Kitty wondered if it was too late to make a break for it.

It was clear that these men had captured her father, and Kitty hoped she could meet up with him before it was too late. She might be able to help him escape. With a plan already starting to form in her mind, Kitty increased her stride and pulled a rather surprised Mr. Gray along behind her.

"We must be quiet now," she whispered, "I think I heard someone in the kitchen."

Kitty and her companion quickly ran into the street and climbed into the car waiting for them. There were two other men already in the car: one was Bill, and the other made Kitty's blood run cold. It was George Stateman, the man who swore he would do everything to destroy Kitty's father.

Both men barely glanced at her as she got in. Stateman sat at the wheel and spoke to her without looking up, saying that he hoped she didn't mind a police chase on her first day. It seemed that they had to accelerate their plans since all of their safe houses were now compromised. Kitty wondered why they didn't just give up and call it quits. If it had been her, she would have walked off the job a long time ago. It seemed like a lot of effort for nothing.

They drove off with the setting sun nearly blinding them and George full into deep thought. Stateman was the chief for good reason. The sway he held over his men was incredible and Kitty found herself almost admiring him. Kitty didn't think she could fight him on his own terms and prayed that someone would rescue her before matters got any worse.

Dan Gray sat beside her, emanating cheerfulness despite being completely silent. He probably didn't want to call attention to himself and get a talking to from Stateman about letting Pete and Tom slip under his radar.

Suddenly he seemed to recall something and sat up straighter. "We left that girl locked up in the basement. Should I go back to get her?"

"And get killed or captured in the attempt? No, thank you."

They all fell silent once more.

Dan wondered why he had ever gotten mixed up in this job and Bill wondered what he could still get out of it. George wondered how he could lose his men and Kitty thought about how she could get out of this mess alive.

Soon enough, George stopped the car near a causeway and they all got out, except for Bill, who drove off. They were left standing, facing the cool ocean breeze. Not fifty yards away floated the white yacht that Kitty had seen earlier.

George waved a large handkerchief and a man on deck returned the gesture. Before long, a dinghy was lowered into the water and came towards the shore.

"It nearly slipped my mind in all the fun, but what was your name?" Kitty turned around quickly to find that George was looking at her with great interest.

Chapter 2

Her mouth went dry and right when she thought that she had been made, he answered his own question.

"Oh, that's right. You're Mary Smith's cousin, the one who did such a grand job up north with those lords. 'Can't Beat You Betty,' right? It's certainly a name to hang on to, my girl. Just do what you did last time and you'll be heading back to London with more money than you can carry. I'll tell you what you have to do once we're onboard."

As he spoke, the row boat came alongside them and Dan had grabbed the prow, holding it steady as Kitty and the rest clamoured in. Kitty sank gratefully onto the seat at the back of the boat. Her luck was holding and she only hoped that it would last long enough for her to figure out what was going on.

She again thought of the prisoner she had met earlier. If Dan was telling the truth, then man and her father were locked up somewhere. The dinghy came closer to the yacht and Kitty read the name 'Lucky Star' on the side. The yacht itself was unremarkable. It looked like any other that sailed along the south coast.

They all climbed aboard and George told her that Dan would show her to Mary's old room, which would now be hers. After he opened the cabin door, he told her that they would have dinner in a few minutes and warned her that the chief didn't like to be kept waiting. Kitty thanked him and he was just about to close the door when Kitty heard someone groaning in pain. At once, she was out in the passage again and quickly asked Dan to take her to see the wounded man. It couldn't be the man she had shot since Dan had told her that he had been taken to the hospital to be treated. Dan was reluctant, but Kitty convinced him eventually. It was a strong man indeed who could withstand the pleadings of a pretty woman. He showed her into a small cabin where a man lay on his stomach moaning. Dan turned him over and Kitty looked down into the face of Paul Trent.

It was lucky for them that Dan had gone back to tell George that Betty was giving their captive some first aid (George hadn't been concerned and had continued into the dining room) for if he hadn't, Dan might have seen the look on Paul's face when he saw "Betty." Paul's expression upon seeing Kitty would have given it away that they had met before and that they were friends.

"Get me something to write on and a pencil," he whispered between groans.

Kitty nodded and started searching the pocket of her jacket, immediately finding a pencil. She held it loosely in her hands as she shifted Paul into a more comfortable position.

Paul's hands were tied together painfully, but Kitty knew better than to ask Dan to loosen them.

She didn't have any paper, but she did have a card.

She took it out of her pocket and put it over his eyes before quickly placing a handkerchief on top just as Dan walked back into the room.

Paul stopped groaning and feigned sleep.

"You must be a vixen in bed with hands like that," Dan sighed. "We'd best hurry or the chief will get in a mood." Dan locked the door of the cabin behind them as they left.

"Give me a second," Kitty said, "I need to freshen up."

She was as good as her word.

When she entered the dining room, she discovered that four men were waiting for her. On the near side of the table, there was George, his face dark with anger, and beside him sat his long time henchman, Louis. On the far side, Dan sat next to a middle-aged man that Kitty had never seen before. He was short and fat, dressed in black from head to toe. Every inch of him emanated a foreign air, and Kitty decided he was probably Dutch. Kitty knew as soon as she stepped into the room that she had walked into the middle of fight. Dan got to his feet, but when the other men didn't he flushed and sat down quickly.

Kitty smiled her brightest smile at him, which seemed to please him immensely. Kitty immediately started thinking of ways to get Dan on her side of things. If they discover who she was, at least she'd have a fighting chance.

"Good evening," she said cheerfully as she sat down in one of the two vacant seats.

The Dutchman looked at her, his brow furrowed and Kitty knew without a doubt that he was the man who had hit her on the back of the head. Luckily, he didn't seem to recognize her.

She was certainly glad that Bill and Jack weren't around.

"To continue what I was saying before the entertainment arrived," the man dressed in black said, his voice rising with anger, "I got that girl and I wanted to bring her here right away—which I had every right to do, seeing that I risked my neck taking her prisoner. But, oh no! That was not good enough! You want to take her to a house in Holt. You say that your men will take care of her and that the danger is here at the yacht—my yacht. I, an honourable man from Rotterdam and famed in that city for my work with diamonds, getting searched by your police? Still, I agreed and see what happens: two of your men get cold feet, talk to the polic—and what do you do? You leave without taking the girl with you. But my spies say that the police didn't raid the house this afternoon and that the search for Arthur Conway was called off because of your telegram saying that he is in Canada. What are you trying to pull?" The man was now shouting and waving wildly, "You try to double-cross me, but only fools toy with Jan van Halle!!"

"Barring the times that he himself is a fool," George broke in with his steeliest voice. "I want no fight with anyone, but if you keep this up, Halle, you'll get what's coming to you. Either you work with me or you deal with the business end of my gun. Take it or leave it."

Van Halle looked at George for a long minute and then his eyes dropped and an audible sigh of relief broke around the table. No one spoke and only the wind and the sea made any noise in the small room.

The two men sat down and began eating. The Dutchman turned

to Kitty and asked her if she would be any good for the job. When she started work, she knew that he would still be just as sure that George was double-crossing him, but he wouldn't be able to overrule the other three that were in favour of her working with them.

Kitty smiled at him, "I am able to work whenever you require my services. I don't care how long it takes. I will get the job done." She desperately hoped that her companion would tell her what exactly what her job entailed, but he only frowned.

"No need for that. You can't start until first light anyway. You had better get some shut-eye after your long journey," George said quickly. "Best hasten off, now. We have other things to discuss."

She gave a quiet good-night as she walked out of the room, but only Dan responded in a rather morose tone.

As soon as she closed the door, she put her ear to it to try and catch what was being said. She could only hear a quiet murmur, but then the foreigner started shouting again and she heard his words as clearly as if she'd been standing next to him.

"I will not let that man off this boat! I have had him off six months and he will only gain his freedom when I am sailing for the East Indies. You can keep Conway, but that man is mine. In two days' time, I will have my millions and you'll be richer, provided you don't double-cross me."

George said something that made the Dutchman shout in anger, "You wouldn't dare. I'll kill you myself, if you do."

That was the last thing Kitty heard properly. After that, they spoke softly and Kitty, afraid of being caught, returned to her cabin. She lay down in her bunk, fully dressed, wondering if she could swim to the shore in the dark, to an unknown location on the coast. She put the foolhardy idea out of her mind and before she knew it, she was fast asleep, even when the yacht erupted into chaos.

It was only three hours after Kitty had left for dinner that Paul

Chapter 2

Trent escaped his bonds, searched a certain gentleman's cabin, jumped overboard, and promptly swam for the shore.

The watch and the bridge saw him within moments and sounded the alarm. In a moment, George and the other three were on deck. They had still been trying to choose a plan of action. Even though they emptied their guns into the sea, they were sure that Paul had escaped. The criminals eventually returned to the table and were still there when the sun rose the next morning. They were certainly in better spirits than the night before and they shook hands all around, telling each other that in a few short hours they would be rich men and never have to work another day in their lives.

Chapter Three

Charles Devonport arrived back at Dark Gate at eight o'clock sharp. James came to the door promptly and looked most surprised.

"Why Mr. Devonport, I thought you and Mr. Trent had followed Master Conway and his daughter to Canada."

"Oh," Charles cried in excitement, "they had turned up?"

"Yes, it seems that there was a problem with one of the mines that Master Conway had to attend to in person. He sent a telegram asking Mistress Katherine as well as yourself and Mr. Trent to follow at once. It seems that the telegram was sent to the wrong address and so it only arrived yesterday afternoon. The police have called off the search, but you and Trent had disappeared. Another telegram arrived later, saying that you and Trent were in Canada and that I was to send the servants on their holiday as we would not be returning until autumn."

Charles stared at James, his face blank.

"Is something wrong, Mr. Devonport?"

"Get me some coffee and something to eat. Bring it to me in the library and bring those wires and the mail that has arrived since Mr. Conway left."

"Certainly, sir. I apologize, sir, but the servants are already away, so the library is a bit dustier than I would like." James bowed and departed, wondering at the strange behaviour of the upper class.

The first thing Charles did when he went into the library was ring 'White Hall 1212.' His dialogue was short and he was not pleased when he hung up the phone. He rang again, but the conversation was even shorter the second time. Charles gave up and waited for his breakfast. He knew that George Stateman had orchestrated this entire debacle. Somehow the man had gotten the police to stop searching and ruined all of Charles efforts to get them to keep going. Added to that was the fact that Scotland Yard was upset with him, demanding that he pay for the wild goose chase he'd sent them on. Charles was getting hot around his collar.

He felt like a fool, knew he was a fool, and swore that he would get to the bottom this by himself— regardless of what the police did or didn't do. For all he knew, Arthur Conway was halfway to the moon as George Stateman's prisoner. His thoughts were interrupted as James came in with his breakfast and a pile of letters. James placed everything on the table beside Charles and was about to leave when Charles asked him what Mr. Conway had done the morning he'd left. James told him about the letter and the missing card.

Charles listened to him without speaking and then said, "James, you've served in the military, haven't you?"

"Indeed, I have, sir."

"Would you be willing to carry a gun again?'

"I would shoot it, if need be."

"Good man. Now, I have a plan." Charles went on to tell James everything that had transpired. He was surprised when James' formal manner dissolved into angry concern for his employer.

"So, Arthur is still in the hands of that rogue."

"Yes, he is," was the grim reply, "but if you help me, he won't be for much longer."

"Tell me what I must do and it will be done."

"I just need to ask you a few questions first. Did you see any strange lorries around the house?"

"I don't think—Oh, wait a minute. I did see one come down the road the other day. It had a bunch of fishing supplies and it headed down very near to the sea. I spoke to them to make sure they didn't fish in the manor's waters. There were three of them and one was a foreigner dressed in black. He replied that it was a free country and he could do as he liked. Arthur gave them permission to do as they liked. They worked until it got dark."

"Did the truck stay there the entire time?"

"No, it went away and returned to pick up the men later."

"That must be the same truck that Paul and I followed. I wonder what happened to him. I hope he is all right," Charles said as he pushed away the remains of his breakfast and started opening the mail.

"Did it turn up this morning?"

"No, but if it does, what will we do, Sir?"

"We'll think of something, and you don't have to use 'Sir' when we're alone like this. I know Mr. Conway let's you call him Arthur, so you can do this much, at least."

"As you wish. Should I fetch my old gun from my quarters?"

"Yes, do that."

When James returned with his gun, Charles was already on the letters that had arrived that morning. It had been delivered by hand and was addressed to Charles. He read it twice before handing it to James. It read:

Charles,

You're very lucky that Miss Conway and that fool Paul Trent have better luck than you or else they would be needing the surgeon.

James looked up, "He's referring to you getting shot, correct?"

"Yes, he is," Charles replied, "but it wasn't really anything to be concerned about. It just needed a few stitches and I was right as rain. Keep reading."

It would be best if you took a holiday, now. I hear the south of France is lovely this time of year. It would be unfortunate if Mr. Conway met with an accident because you dallied in England. Enclosed are three tickets. I expect them to be used.

George Stateman & Co.

James handed it back without a word. "I can't really make heads or tails of it. I imagine that Stateman fears you interfering with his plans and wants you out of the country, but I doubt that Mr. Conway is in mortal danger. Stateman wouldn't go that far. It's too risky, especially if he gets caught."

"But, James," Charles said, "If he's already willing to threaten me like this, there's no telling how far he will go. If he's backed into a corner the way I think he is, who knows what he is capable of."

"Well, there is one thing in your favour. It doesn't seem that he has either Miss Conway or Mr. Trent, but if he doesn't, where are they?"

Chapter 3

Before Charles could answer, the phone rang.

He picked up. "This is Dark Gate. Who is this?"

"Is there a Charles Devonport there? It is urgent," said the voice on the other end of the line.

"This is he. What do you want?"

"A man was brought in this morning to the ward at King Hymns. I am the sister in charge. We haven't been able to identify him yet, but he kept asking for a Charles Devonport at Dark Gate. Would you be willing to come down here?"

"I think I can guess without seeing him. If I'm right, his name is Paul Trent. What on Earth happened to him? Is he all right?"

"He was hit by a car early this morning and a passerby brought him in. Will you be coming down to see him?"

"I'll be there as soon as I can."

"I'll be waiting for you then, sir. Have a good day."

Charles put down the receiver and turned to James. "Paul is in the hospital and I still have no idea what is going on."

He wasn't any wiser when he came out of Paul's room an hour later. Paul was on painkillers and kept rambling on about a rabbit hiding in Kitty's flower garden.

"Was he your friend?" the sister in charge asked.

"Yes, but it seems he is having trouble focusing. He didn't tell me anything worth mentioning. Did he have anything on him? He was supposed to be with another friend of ours and I need to find her."

"There was a white card in his pocket. He was sopping wet when he was brought in, so the card was a little wet as well. We were afraid he met catch hypothermia for awhile there, but he seems to be warm enough now."

"Could you bring me the card?"

The nurse returned a moment later with the card.

Charles thanked her and said that he would return the next day to check on his friend. With that said, Charles walked out and went to the car where James was waiting.

"Any luck?" James asked absently.

"Maybe, but I don't know. I got this card. It must be the one that was lost earlier. I wonder how Paul got hold of it. If he was lucid, things would a sight easier."

"Well, I can confirm that it is indeed the missing card. It looks like there is something inside. Open it up, will you?"

With a nod, Charles nervously tore open the end of the card. As he did so, something fell out into his lap. He picked it up and held it out to James. It looked like a strongbox key, but not of a design Charles was familiar with.

"What," Charles asked in wonder, "is this doing in there? Who would put a key in a card and why?" Charles squinted at it. "There's something written on it, but I can't read it."

"Let me see," James said, reaching for the key, "It says, 'Made in Holland.'"

"So it's a key to a strongbox in Holland? The boys at the Yard will never believe this one. Let's go back to Dark Gates and see if those 'fishermen' have turned up today." Charles said as he started the car and headed back towards the Conway home.

The weather took a turn for the worse and the road was soon covered with water and fog. Even with the lights on, Charles could only see a few yards ahead of the car. Without even realizing it, they were soon lost. It was only after they had been driving for over an hour that they realized that they should have long since reached Dark Gates and were lost.

They continued down the road, hoping to find a village or town where they could get directions. As they continued driving and no buildings came into sight, Charles started wondering how they would get out of the fog if the car ran out of gas.

James reassured him that they would reach a town before that happened. Before Charles could reply, a strange sound pierced through the dense mist. It wasn't the sound any human could make. The strange, burbling noise reminded Charles of a large glob of slime, slithering across the British landscape.

Charles stopped the car and they both sat in silence, listening to the sound. It went on for two minutes before it was interrupted by a dull explosion followed by an eerie silence.

"What was that?" James asked, pale as a sheet.

"I don't know, but we had better find out," Charles replied, his face hard.

"It sounded like it came from beside us, so we'll have to leave the car behind. We had best hurry. People might be hurt."

James and Charles jumped out of the car. James still looked shaken, but his colour was improved. He asked, "Do you think we should bring anything, sir? We'd better be prepared."

"Prepared for what?"

"They say that there are strange happenings in these parts when the fog rolls in like this."

"Don't tell me you're afraid of an old ghost story?"

"Far from it, sir. I was only informing you that strange things have happened around here. We might want to head for the coast. I know that the ships will be having a tough time in this weather. That Dutchman's yacht, 'Lucky Star,' should be nearby. We could ask them to lend a hand if need be."

"Hopefully, they aren't the ones who need help."

They walked along in silence, heading in the direction of the noise, crossing a field before reaching the water. They stood and looked into the clouds of mist that billowed above the waves.

"I wonder what that noise was."

"It might have been that yacht hitting a sandbar or something. The shallows around here are rather tricky to navigate. They might have run into the Fens and gotten stuck."

"But the sound was so drawn out, that couldn't be it. Plus, there is also the matter of that explosion."

"I don't know, sir. I have never heard that sound before, so it is difficult to approximate what could have caused it."

Seeing that they could go no farther and that the whole countryside lay beneath the strange stillness of the fog, they started back to the car. Both were so immersed in their own thoughts that they didn't keep track of where they were walking.

Before long, they were again lost in the fog. They tried to listen to the sound of the sea to reorient them, but the sound surrounded them, seeming to come everywhere and nowhere all at once. They stayed together, fearing that if they separate, they'd never find each other in the fog. After half an hour of wandering, they finally found the road. Right as they located their car, they heard six gunshots.

With James' gun and excitement coursing through their veins, they took off down the road in the direction of the shots.

"It seems we're in the thick of something other than fog." As Charles spoke, there was the sound of more shots to the right of them, coming from the sea.

It was then that a car appeared out of the mist in front of them. They both hit the ground and started scrambling forward while trying to keep their heads down. James was leading in front. Charles' wound felt like it had reopened and he swerved to the side as he pressed his fingers to it, trying to determine if it was bleeding. It was a lucky thing he did because if he hadn't moved a bullet would have hit him in the chest instead of whistling past his ear.

Charles and James dove into the ditch, pressing themselves to the ground as flat as they could. They could hear the men talking. It was a foreigner speaking, "Kill him! Do it quickly before the police get here. Leave those fools alone! We don't have time to deal them."

There was the heart-stopping crack of a pistol.

"Is it done?" Asked the foreigner.

"Back of the head, just like you ordered," came the cool reply. That voice stopped Charles from tackling the foreigner to the ground. He would know that voice anywhere.

It was Kitty's. He saw her figure leave the car followed by the foreigner's and disappear into the hedge. Charles got to his feet weakly and tried to think of a plan to follow Kitty and ask her if she'd gone mad. But he didn't have time to stumble after her, for a blue-coated coast guard came across the road and snapped a pair of cuffs on Charles' wrists, holding them fast.

"Give me any more trouble and I'll crack one over your head." He blew his whistle and an answering whistle drifted back to them. Charles found his voice.

"You're making a mistake, sir! I'm not your man. He ran into those hedges barely a minute ago."

"That's what they all say," replied the man, but he started to look doubtful when the shooting started again in the distance. He refused to investigate and told Charles to sit down and keep quiet.

Charles told him that there was a wounded man in the car and that he needed to give the man medical attention. They both went to the car. There lay a man in shabby clothes with a dirty, unkempt beard. His face was thin and his eyes were closed. After a quick examination, Charles found only a bruise and no bullet wound. The man had been knocked unconscious, not shot.

Why had Kitty said that she had shot him when she hadn't? What was she doing with the foreigner? Charles had no doubt that it had been Kitty, but it didn't look like she was being forced to do anything. They wouldn't give a prisoner a gun, so that was out of the equation.

These questions swirled around Charles' mind, but he was only left with more questions. The coast guard made the man as comfortable as possible, linked Charles' handcuffs the car, and disappeared for a into the fog. James had just climbed out from the ditch to rescue Charles when the coast guard came back with a man from Scotland Yard. It was fortunate for James and Charles that the latter was recognized as a fellow officer. The man from Scotland Yard assured the coast guard that Charles had not yet departed from the straight and narrow, and that his friend was assuredly just as innocent. Apparently, the officers were searching for some smugglers. The police had managed to wound one, but the criminals had avoided capture.

They hadn't recovered any goods whatsoever and the evidence to prove that they were conducting illegal trades with the Continent was circumstantial at best.

The chief agreed with the constable from the Yard that Charles and James had nothing to do with the whole thing, but they still had to be taken in for questioning. After that, they would be free to do as they pleased. They all made their way to the nearest village where James and Charles gave a detailed account of what they had done all morning and their occupations and permanent addresses. They were allowed to go free and the unconscious man was taken to the hospital.

Chapter 3

The doctor reported that the man was severely malnourished and was suffering from acute sleep deprivation. He wasn't to be disturbed until the doctors gave the all-clear.

Charles and James returned to their car, uncertain as to what they should now do. The constable from the Yard knocked on the window and asked if he could lend a hand.

"If I understand you correctly, you've gotten yourself into a mess of trouble. Until that man is whole and well, I've naught to do, but twiddle my thumbs."

James and Charles exchanged looks.

They burst out laughing and Charles replied: "Well, if you want, you're welcome to join us. I suppose you heard about Paul."

The man nodded, "The staff told me that he was resting and couldn't take visitors until this evening. Why don't you tell me what kind of mess I've just walked into?"

Charles filled in Constable Ross with the details as they drove back to Dark Gates.

"It's surely been a strange business from the start. I'd wager good money that George Stateman's behind all of this—but that isn't what concerns me. There is the matter of Miss Conway running around with those thugs. Nobody seems to know what she is doing. If I had to guess, I'd say that she was trying to free her father, but something else might be going on as well. And then there's that key. Would you mind letting me have a look at it?"

Charles took it out and handed it to Ross. "If you have any ideas, tell me. I gave up trying a long time ago"

"I don't know what exactly it unlocks, but I know what it is." Ross pointed to the end of the key. "It's for a small safe, definitely Dutch. This shape was usually for a small lockbox used by ship captains and little old ladies. It's been years since I've seen one. They were only popular during the war, but haven't been used much since."

Charles smiled. "It's not terribly helpful information, but it's something. So we know that there is a wartime Dutch safe that's too small to fit Arthur Conway into."

James interrupted: "Let's get some food and see if we can think up an explanation for this mess between the three of us while we eat."

They soon pulled up to Dark Gates and the sun appeared to greet them. The fog that had been so dense earlier that day had all but disappeared until not a trace of it remained. James led the way into the house with Charles and Ross following after him.

＊＊＊

Kitty woke up early following her night's rest. She wasn't sure that she liked being on the boat, especially since she did not know what she was supposed to do or who she was supposed to be. She didn't think about it long. She jumped to her feet and silently made her way to the door and listened. The passageway was silent. The only sound she heard was the rhythmic thump of her heart. She opened the door and paused to listen.

This time she heard voices in the dining cabin. She crept up to the door and put her ear to the door. She heard the Dutchman and George Stateman's voice, but they were too low for her to tell what they were saying. She wondered if they had been speaking the entire time she had been asleep.

Next, she went to the cabin where Paul had been kept prisoner and found it open. The door had been forced open. She saw that he had written a message on the wall with the pencil. It read 'Free. Will call police.' She wondered if he had written anything else and started looking around. Just when she was about to give up, she found an old book hidden in some clothes. It wasn't a large book, and when she opened it something fell out.

It was a photo of the man she had rescued two days ago, only he was younger and fitter here. She flipped it over. 'V. Herlache 1939' had been written on the back. With her hands trembling with excitement, Kitty opened the book. It had to be the diary of V. Herlache and this mystery would certainly be resolved within its pages.

She read page after page, drinking in every bit of information. She learned that Herlache had been a businessman in Rotterdam. He was a diamond cutter for one of the largest diamond companies in Europe.

The diary mentioned a fellow manager named 'Van Halle' whom Herlache disliked.

The tenth of May, 1940, was written in red ink and underlined. The entry read:

> At 0400 hours this morning, the Germans crossed the border into my country. God help Her.

The next entry was May the fourteenth:

> Men are running everywhere, fleeing for their lives. No one knows when the Germans will enter this, my fair city of Rotterdam. Some say tonight, others say tomorrow. I say that it does not matter. My city is dead. Whether the Germans march on her corpse today or the next day matters little. I am alone, having paid the men who worked under me. I am uncertain what to do with the diamonds. Van Halle has left me. Someone said that he left with the British. Here I am, alone in the shop with millions of pounds worth of diamonds sitting in a steel container while my city lies in ruins. My fair Rotterdam, what have you done to deserve this?

Kitty turned the page and went on reading without taking any note of the noise around her. George and Van Halle were shouting orders on deck, some in English and some in Dutch.

The next entry was May the sixteenth:

I have left my country for the first time in my life, perhaps never to return. I write here what has transpired, so that when I must judge myself in the years to come, I will know why things have turned out this way.

The world may say that my duty was to stay and safeguard the diamonds, but the government has requested that I turn them over so that they can be used to fund the rebuilding of my homeland. I was overjoyed, but I must deliver them to the minister in London. I asked for help, but it was refused. I had to do the impossible alone.

The police had fled and people wondered aimlessly in the streets. These things are well-documented and I will not linger on the horrors of those days. I and a few friends got a boat and were escaping in the canal when we heard that the Germans were going to drain it to put out the fires. We put the diamonds in a secret safe aboard the ship.

The next entry was on the twentieth of May:

It was a near thing that I wasn't jailed. The minister said that I had carried out my duty regardless of whether the diamonds could be recovered or not. I wish to write here what I told him before the words leave my mind and I forget the details.

When we were a day at sea, a German gunboat same alongside our starboard side and commanded us to return to port or they would open fire. We convinced them that our boat wouldn't survive a trip back and they told us to abandon ship, so they could sink our vessel. They claimed that they would recover our life rafts if we cooperated. I convinced my friends to take one of the lifeboats while I remained onboard. They went reluctantly and the gunboat opened fire. Part of the sail caught aflame and it took me hours to put it out. By the time I had, the boat was very low in the water. I had been carried within sight of the Norfolk coast, but I feared that the ship wouldn't last until morning.

It is only by God's grace that I was wrong. Come morning, the boat was still barely afloat. The rudder was destroyed and the sails were gone. I still had the key to the safe, but the cabin was inaccessible. I waited for the tide to be with me and then swam to shore as the boat sank below the water. I was immediately arrested as a German spy, but the Dutch minister came from London and freed me. What I write here is the truth about what happened to the Queen's diamonds. If I live through these times, I swear to recover them from the sea.

I maintain that every word I wrote here is true.

V. Herlache

Kitty closed the book and wondered what her part was to play in this mystery. She already assumed that she would be going down in a diving suit to retrieve the diamond.

She didn't fear the job as it wasn't the first time she would be diving, but she did fear George Stateman remembering who she really was. The only thing she had to do was get this job done as quickly as possible and everything would be all right. Still, she wondered how her father had gotten mixed up into this whole thing.

She remembered a few months ago that a foreigner arrived at Dark

Gates, requesting a loan to reclaim something he wouldn't name. He had spoken with her father all through the night and had left the next morning. Her father had said that the man was a friend from the war who had needed some money.

Kitty finally connected the dots: the foreigner that had spoken to her father was the wild, unshaven man she had met the other day. She understood now what the Lucky Star was doing. They were trying to recover millions of dollars worth of diamonds, including one of the largest high-quality diamonds on record—and she was supposed to help. But she didn't have long to think. Someone knocked on her door and informed her that the chief wanted her on deck, at once.

She replied that she would be up shortly, quickly put back the diary where she had found it, and hastened up to the deck where she was greeted by Van Halle and Dan. The latter gave her a cheery, "Good morning."

Van Halle gave her a dark look and wanted to know if she was any good at swimming.

Kitty told him that she would not be here if she was not and that Mary Smith had some sense.

"Well, I don't mind telling you," Van Halle said with a frown, "I wouldn't be caught in one of those things, no matter how much you paid me. They're dangerous, but you'll probably be all right with Dan. He is one of the best when it comes to those death traps." he pointed to the iron diving helmet. "Between the two of you, we should be finished the whole thing and sailing away by tomorrow. Get your suit on. I don't like it when the weather gets like this. Let's hope the mist doesn't get too thick out here." By the time Dan got Kitty into her diving suit, they could no longer see the shoreline.

Just before Dan put on her headgear, she asked him how the prisoners were and where George was. To answer the first, he responded that Paul Trent had escaped in the night. George and his henchman, Louis, had gone ashore to try and capture him and keep an eye on the police to prevent any surprise attacks on the yacht.

Chapter 3

When they were both ready, they went down together, lowered in with ropes. Kitty was in a mood and would have preferred to give herself up, had she not had a braver side that overruled her fear. Before she knew it, they had reached the sea bed and she was having the time of her life. It was beautiful in a way that she had never considered possible. She would have dallied the morning away watching the fish swim by if it hadn't be for Dan taking her hand. They walked towards a large, dark shape in the water.

When they were within a few feet of it, it became apparent that this was the boat that Herlache had written about. It lay on its side, half-destroyed and riddled with bullet holes. They went inside and made their way below deck. They found the cabin that Herlache had spoken about and Dan gestured for her to try to squeeze into the room to retrieve the diamonds inside. Kitty tried, but discovered the that collapsed space was too small for even someone of her stature to get through. Dan motioned for them to return to the boat.

Kitty, for one, was not sorry when the diving helmet was removed and she could breathe fresh air once more. Dan was explaining to an enraged Van Halle that Kitty couldn't make into the hole where the diamonds were.

"You think I am a fool!" The foreigner cried, "you English, you try and make a fool of me, but you won't. I will not wait any longer. The safe comes up immediately and we will blow that ship to bits. It's not like anyone knows what we're up to out here."

Van Halle put Dan in charge of setting the explosives to break up the boat. They needed to surface the safe with the diamonds. Kitty followed him down into the heart of the small vessel and stopped to turn a key in lock. Peering through the doorway, Kitty had to use all her strength not to cry out. Inside the room where they kept the prisoners was none other than her father, bound hand and foot, but there was a light in his eyes. Beside him sat the man she knew to be Victor Herlache.

Van Halle's face worked with rage as he laid eyes on his two prisoners. His voice was hard as he said, "Arthur Conway, you are a rich man, so unless you make Stateman and I five hundred thousand pounds richer, I promise that you will never see the light of day again. It is true that tonight I will have diamonds worth twenty million pounds, but I have never been one to turn my back on easy money and I never will." He continued with obvious venom, "It is unfortunate, but you, my dear Vincent, will remain with us indefinitely. Such is life."

"You just wait," Arthur cried, his voice catching on the last word. "You will never get away with this. You'll be lucky if you don't get the noose. You can talk till you're blue in the face, but you will never get a penny out of me."

Kitty stayed out of the room, just in case her father gave some sign he recognized her.

"Come, Vincent," Van Halle continued, ignoring Arthur's outburst, "You have work to do."

He grabbed Vincent's upper arm, not bothering to help the man to his feet and proceeded to drag him along by his arm without even looking back. It was all Vincent could do to scramble to his feet. After months of captivity and starvation, putting up a fight was the last thing on his mind. As Van Halle turned to lock the door, Kitty handed Vincent a knife she had pinched earlier and he hid it under his coat, a distant sheen of hope flickering in his sunken eyes.

Van Halle turned around and led them all back on deck without noticing anything amiss. Dan walked up to them, his youthful face alight with excitement.

"Well, Van, everything is set for the big bang. I'll have to be taken ashore to set it off, so this fog is a real stroke of luck. No one will see what we're up to and people will just think all the noise is an old mine going off.

"Good, that's splendid," the man in black smirked, rubbing his large hands together. "All we need is dear, old George and then we can go ashore."

Chapter 3

"Here I am," came Stateman's hard tones as he came walking along the misty deck, "and I bring good news. The police are still in the dark as to what we are trying to do. Paul Trent is in the hospital and can't remember a thing. With any luck, the job will be finished before they get wise to it."

George was soon informed of their plan to blow the hull of the old ship to get to the diamonds.

"With a few precise detonations, the safe containing the diamonds should still be intact," Dan continued, "and it will only take a few hours to break it open."

It was agreed that George should take the 'Lucky Star' out to sea and return once the explosives had been blown in an hour or so. The others, including Vincent Herlache and another henchman, would go ashore and control the operation from there. Kitty was glad that she had a chance of getting ashore because she had a feeling that George was on the verge of remembering who she was—or did already, and was keeping quiet for some unknown reason. After landing, Dan readied all his materials and everything was prepared in short order. Herlache had been left in the dinghy, by Kitty saw him climb out as Dan sent the signal to detonate the explosives. The siren wailed, high and eerie, for two whole minutes as the final calibrations were made and the explosives were armed.

Van Halle jumped when the final explosion shot a column of water into the air. When he turned round, he saw the figure of Vincent running for the nearest hedge over the marshy land. With a cry of rage, he set off in pursuit just as a cry came through the fog.

"Close in men! We have them cornered."

Kitty, afterwards, could not remember anything of the next hour. All she knew was that a pale-faced Dan had handed her a pistol and that when she thought that Van Halle would shoot Vincent where he sat in the driver's seat of the car, she had run in and shot into the seat cushion, saying that she got him through the head. It was a near thing, but Van Halle, distracted by his fear for his own safety, took her at her word and with Dan's help, they were able to get back to the boat in the ensuing confusion and make good their escape. The details of the events were forgotten though, as the strain of the past three days—as well as the overwhelming shock she experienced from the explosion and nearly killing a man—were too much; Kitty passed out, much to the chagrin of her partners in crime.

Dan carried her, even though the foreigner had ordered him to leave her behind, but Dan snapped, "If she is left behind, then I'll stay with her and we will all go to prison. For us, life's luck can change in a matter of hours, so don't go acting as if you've got your jewels just yet. It's about time our luck changed, so don't think everything will just go your way."

Except things did. They found the boat as soon as the mist cleared and Dan went down in his diving suit to retrieve the safe. In a s short time, the rusty safe was brought out of the water and placed on the deck by a small crane. The men began the process of breaking into it.

They were done with working in the dark of night. This was it; Either they made it or they didn't. It was only a matter time before the coast guards came and asked them what they were doing. If that happened, the jig was up.

Kitty didn't come to until late in the afternoon. Even then, she lay on her bunk looking up at the ceiling, wondering what had happened. Eventually, she remembered and jumped up, running to the door. She had to try to stop these men. If she could, it would only be a little while before Charles knew the truth and would come to her aid. She tried the door. It was locked.

She was a prisoner. She looked around the room wildly, hunting with her eyes for something to force the door open, but there wasn't anything she could use. Then she noticed that the porthole had not been locked.

Chapter 3

She could squeeze through and then swim ashore. Even if it was too far, she could always grab onto one of the many ropes on the side of the vessel and climb back onto the boat. No sooner did she think of this then she acted, flinging the porthole open and looking out at the sea. The top of the tallest waves were not more than a few feet away.

Kitty put her head and shoulders through and there was an awful moment where she was halfway through, neither in nor out, flailing to get free. Then she was in the cold waters going farther and farther down. Her tumble had been ill-timed, and a wave had unexpectedly risen to meet her as she took a deep breath. She cut to the surface with a gasp, her lungs burning as they filled with the life-giving air once more. The setting sun reflected into her eyes and gave Kitty her bearings, but she couldn't help ignoring the picturesque setting. She was too adrenalized to even notice the time of day, but she noticed the sails of the 'Lucky Star' going up.

She watched the white cloth rise higher and higher, distracted from her purpose. She forgot that the sails unfurling also meant the ship was about to leave her behind in the water and she was not the best of swimmers. By the time she realized her mistake, it was too late. The boat had swung away from her. Kitty started after it as fast as she could and even shouted from them to stop, but she knew it was useless.

The yacht did turn around, but it whipped past her, its motors screaming in the evening air. Kitty grabbed at the ropes along the side the ship, but the cold made her uncoordinated and the ropes, slick with water, were moving by too fast for her to get a good grip.

In a few moments, she was hit by the terrible wake of the yacht and she was sent careening in every direction it seemed. She managed to fight her way free of the turbulent waters, but only with great difficulty. A wave of fatigue washed over her and Kitty fought off the exhaustion as she fought to stay afloat.

The whole world seemed to be sliding back and forth, twisting up and over her as wave after wave buried her beneath the sea. Kitty felt as though she was trapped in a nightmare, but knew it would not be long before it was over. Her strength was quickly running out. It seemed as though every part of her body became a weight, dragging her down into the darkness.

Her hair hung like a wet curtain overtop of her face, making it nearly impossible to breathe. Cold hands pawed at her clothes, grasping at her limbs, trying to pull her to the seafloor. Her ears were ringing. Kitty couldn't even hear the crash of the waves or the cry of the gulls, only the unceasing alarm in her mind.

Her mind started to wander and it became difficult to focus on staying afloat. She remembered a story from her childhood that her father had once told her about a knight who lived in the sea and rode stallions made of foam and water. He saved fishermen lost at sea and guiding lost souls to their rest. Kitty imagined that he rode towards her, now, riding a chariot of sapphire and emerald, pulled by a team of white horses with lightning for eyes.

She even thought she saw a woman with hair like the sun standing beside him, reaching towards her.

Kitty stopped moving. What was the point? Here she was, safe and warm in her mother's arms, but why couldn't she rest? There was someone calling her in the distance. It was a man's voice, but not her father's. She wished she could swim a little longer, so she could see who it is. His voice was nice.

But she was just so very, very tired and the thundering in her ears was getting louder. She gave one last look at her sky, the sun sleepily dipping beneath the horizon. Then the sea closed over her and she slid down into the endless dark, the sweet, forgetfulness of eternal night.

She did not later remember the strong arms that hoisted her out of the sea or Charles' face, pale as a sheet as he swam with her in his arms. She did not recall James giving her first aid or how the hands of her family held her all through the night.

Chapter Four

Arthur Conway, architect of Conway Enterprises and self-made millionaire, rolled across the floor of the cabin in which he was held. He had been trying to loosen the ropes that bound him for hours, but they would not budge. It was only when he heard someone approaching that he stilled. Quickly, he righted himself and sat up, facing the door. Dan came in quickly and shut the door behind him. Neither man spoke.

Arthur knew from the look on the man's face that something was wrong. At last, when Dan spoke, his voice was hoarse with worry and tight with anxiety.

"Sir, you may think you know all you need to, but there are things a man keeps hidden in his heart. My actions may be found wanting and my character lacking, but I always swore that if I had to choose between my livelihood and a man's life, I wouldn't forsake my fellow man. That being said," he worried his lip nervously, "I would like to help you escape. It just doesn't sit right with me, killing a man with a family."

"Well," Arthur said, his suspicions laid aside, "I doubt that they would go so far as that, but if we get out of this together, you won't find yourself in prison and you may even get a reward for your services. However, I've never helped a man jump ship and I don't intend to start."

Dan went red all the way up to the tips of his ears. "Sir, do not think ill of me for deserting. I have not chosen to turn tail at the first sign of trouble for things have never been better than they are right now. I didn't mind this job, even if I didn't care for my employers, but them almost leaving that girl behind certainly changes matters."

"What girl?" Arthur cried, his heart already supplying the answer.

"The girl with the glasses and blonde hair."

Dan told Arthur all he knew of the girl, even her nickname. Once Dan had said everything, Arthur told him to return to his duties and do what he could to help himself. The moment the door closed, Arthur started fighting his bonds with renewed vigour. Kitty was in danger, especially if she had tried to swim for shore. He had to get free. However, he was not left alone long; Soon, the door opened again and Van Halle walked in. He seemed ill at ease and jumpy. He started to talk before the door was shut.

"Mr. Conway, I am, as you know, a gentleman and a citizen of the noble city of Rotterdam. I am of the opinion that you and I could be great friends, all things considered."

Arthur said not a word. What was Van Halle's game? Arthur was sure there was a catch—some treachery about to be committed.

"We are in similar situations I believe. See, I am a sheep among the wolves as are you."

"Except one of us is only wearing sheep's clothing, right Van Halle?"

Van Halle's mouth tightened at the remark, but he did not comment on it. An ugly gleam came into his eyes.

"To put it plainly, Mr. Conway, I find I am in need of your aid. Help me and I can give you your freedom."

"You and your partner, George Stateman, can rot in Hell for all I care. You get into bed with a snake; you suffer the consequences. Is that plain enough for you?"

Chapter 4

"I'll throw in a third of the diamonds."

"Never," Arthur said.

Van Halle began to sweat profusely, "Two-thirds of the diamonds, the yacht and your life. Surely that is enough to appease you."

"There is nothing you can give me that I want. An honest man does not go into business for himself and you are the most self-serving waste of humanity that I have ever had the misfortune of meeting. You will leave me now to my thoughts."

Van Halle gave Arthur's ribs a vicious kick and went on his way, saying only that Arthur would be dead in twenty-four hours. Arthur wondered, not for the first time, what had happened that was causing the rats to come to the prisoner for help. They say that "thieves fall out; honest men come into their own." And Arthur hoped it was true. He wondered if Stateman would be paying him a visit soon and continued to pull at the ropes. But in only a few minutes, the door was unlocked yet again and George Stateman entered the room.

"Well," Arthur asked in a quiet voice, "what can I do for you, George?"

"Help me," came the equally soft response. "See, I'm in a bad way. If you can help me, I'll take a single diamond and you will never see me again. I have been meaning to tell you this, but it was I who allowed your daughter to escape."

"Oh yes, you helped her get out the frying pan right into the fire. No, George, maybe there was a time when I would have forgiven you and renewed our past... partnership, but never again. If you get out now, while the going's good, then I won't pursue you. The police will leave you well-enough alone provided you never darken these shores again."

George turned slowly and left the cabin, lost deep in thought, not even bothering to lock the door. Where could his tethered prisoner go anyway? Night came and still Arthur fought the ropes that held him fast. It took every ounce of his strength, but at long last, he broke through the bonds.

Everything was still. It was morning, but the sun had yet to rise. Arthur snuck around the ship, going from cabin to cabin and even to the deck, but there was not a soul to be found. Feeling brave, he even dared to call out, but no one answered his shout.

There was only the ship cat, pattering alongside him, guarding the sole occupant of the ship it seemed. Arthur looked down at it and found a letter attached to its collar.

In a moment, he had it in his hands and read the note. It read:

> Gentlemen,
> I and the rest of the crew have decided that we've done more than our fair share of the work. We have taken our pay.

Dan Gray and several of the crewmen signed it, so that explained where they were, but where had Van Halle, George and Louis gotten to? Arthur shook his head and decided not to dwell on it without getting something to eat first.

But he didn't dine alone. The ship cat turned up and between the two of them, they ate a first-class meal of cold chicken sausage, tomatoes, fish, and coffee for himself and milk for the cat. Following that, he found the smashed up safe on deck, and took an inventory of the diamonds. None of them seemed to be missing. He had figured that Dan wouldn't take any, but why hadn't George or Van Halle plundered the jewels already?

The answer to the mystery came in the form of two notes stashed amongst the precious stones. The first was written by George saying that since the crew had run off, there was no need for him to stay and get all the blame. Apparently, he and Louis would be moving on and they would never meet with Van Halle again. George also expressed a wish to see Arthur again during his travels. It wasn't impossible, but Arthur wondered why George would still be interested in befriending him after this mess.

The second note had been written in three languages. They all roughly translated to say that Van Halle wasn't to blame for any of this and that if the world wasn't such a terrible, heathenish place, he, a God-fearing man, would not be forced to do such things.

Tears of laughter streamed down Arthur's face by the time he finished reading it. He was still laughing about the whole thing when a British gunship drew up alongside the boat in the early hours of the next day, and Charles Devonport leapt from the gunship to the yacht and shook Arthur's hand, telling him that Kitty was safe.

Ross, the constable from the Yard, followed the coast guard to the yacht and took charge of returning the diamonds to the Dutch government.

Ross informed him that he would try to capture Van Halle and Stateman, but as there were no leads, he also told him that they shouldn't get their hopes up just yet.

As Arthur left the yacht with the sleeping cat nestled in his arms, he turned to look at Charles and said, "I don't think I'll be investing in that cruise line after all."

Epilogue

Things were soon back to normal and some ten days later, at Dark Gates, Kitty threw a tea party—having recovered from her near drowning and returned safely to her father. The day was wonderful in the way the weather often is when good news arrives and the house was filled with the smell of the sea and warm sunshine. Everyone was content to merely smell the sea and not go sailing on it quite yet. Arthur was pleased to discover the depths of his manservant's concern for him and that the staunch professionalism could give way to genuine human emotion on occasion.

Vincent Herlache was to return to his former position as a jeweller for the royal family. Paul was still confined to bed rest, but had brokered a compromise that involved his chair being placed outside in the garden amongst his friends. That didn't stop his from complaining about the heat, but his banter reassured them all that he would make a full recovery. Ross had come down and Arthur had asked if either Stateman or Van Halle had been captured yet, to which Ross replied that they had called off the search. It seemed that they had made it to foreign shores and wouldn't be returning any time soon.

As soon as was polite, Kitty got up and went out on the lawn where she was soon joined by Charles a few minutes later.

At last, Kitty broke her silence and spoke first. "Charles, do you think Dan will become respectable? Do you think he'll find an honest occupation?"

"Yes, I am confident that he will." He answered, wondering why he felt jealous of a man he had never met.

There was a long silence, which again, Kitty broke by speaking. "How did you save me? I mean to say, that is, how did you know I was drowning?"

"I didn't know. I spent the whole afternoon with Ross and James before learning the truth of things from Vincent later at the hospital. After that, we got a motorboat and I saw your hair in the water and knew it must be you."

"But how?" She looked up at the tall man beside her, but quickly looked away again. "It might have been seaweed or some such thing. There was no need for you to dive in like that and risk your life."

"How could you say that? The great Katherine Conway comparing her hair to seaweed? I never thought I'd see the day." He smiled at her softly, "There is no hair in the world like yours. I'd know it, even if I were blind."

They continued to walk in silence after that. Kitty looked into the sunset, and after awhile, Charles interrupted her tranquil state.

"Penny for your thoughts."

Kitty looked surprised, but it gave way to a roguish smile and twinkling eyes. "Why, I was thinking of having you fix my garden fence while kitty cat and I tell you how it should be done. I know how much you like to work for pretty women."

"I know. It's a shame there aren't any nearby, but I suppose I could help out kitty—not that much work will get done with you giving the orders." Charles sighed dramatically.

Kitty laughed and gave his arm a light smack. "Silly, old Charles, what would I do without you?" Kitty said as she went to greet her father striding across the lawn towards them.

Charles sighed again and followed her, "What indeed?"

Finis

www.ingramcontent.com/pod-product-compliance
Lightning Source LLC
Chambersburg PA
CBHW020703030726
47498CB00002B/613

* 9 7 8 1 8 9 5 3 8 5 4 3 4 *